The throw was coming in high.

The play was going to be close!

Harlan caught the ball and tried to sweep it down for the tag—all in one motion.

The runner slid hard, taking Harlan's legs out from under him. Harlan landed right on top of the runner, in a cloud of dust.

But the tag was in time!

Harlan jumped up, excited. *"Yeah!"* he shouted.

And then he heard the umpire. *"Safe!!!"*

Harlan jumped around. "What do you mean *'safe'?!"*

"You didn't catch the ball."

*Look for these books about the
Angel Park All-Stars*

SAFE AT FIRST

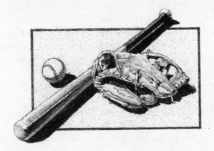

By Dean Hughes

Illustrated by Dennis Lyall

Bullseye Books · Alfred A. Knopf
New York

Library of Congress Cataloging-in-Publication Data
Hughes, Dean, 1943–
Safe at first / by Dean Hughes ; illustrated by Dennis Lyall.
p. cm.—(Angel Park all-stars ; 11)
Summary: The Dodgers are worried about one of their rookies who
keeps messing up for no apparent reason.
ISBN 0-679-81538-4 (pbk.)—ISBN 0-679-91538-9 (lib. bdg.)
[1. Baseball—Fiction.] I. Lyall, Dennis, ill. II. Title.
III. Series: Hughes, Dean, 1943– Angel Park all-stars ; 11.
PZ7.H87312Saf   1991
[Fic]—dc20   90-49992

RL: 4.4
First Bullseye Books edition: May 1991
Manufactured in the United States of America
10 9 8 7 6 5 4 3 2 1

for Elizabeth Tyler

★ 1 ★

Hard Slide

The first runner crossed the plate. The second one powered around third and sprinted toward home.

Harlan Sloan knew he would have a play. He threw his catcher's mask aside and took a step up the line. He was ready to receive the throw and block the plate.

Lian Jie caught the throw from the outfield, spun, and gunned the ball home. Harlan waited. He could hear the runner's steps pounding toward him.

The throw was coming in high.

The play was going to be close!

Harlan caught the ball and tried to sweep it down for the tag—all in one motion.

The runner slid hard, taking Harlan's legs out from under him. Harlan landed right on top of the runner, in a cloud of dust.

But the tag was in time!

Harlan jumped up, excited. *"Yeah!"* he shouted.

And then he heard the umpire. *"Safe!!!"*

Harlan jumped around. "What do you mean *'safe'*?!"

"You didn't catch the ball."

Harlan looked into his mitt. It was empty!

By then Jonathan Swingle, the Dodgers' star pitcher, was running home, screaming, "Behind you, Harlan! Behind you!"

But another runner crossed the plate before Harlan could chase the ball down.

"Harlan, you pulled your glove down too fast," Jonathan told him. "The ball glanced off your mitt. Make sure you catch it before you tag the guy."

Jonathan turned and marched back to the mound. Harlan knew he was mad. At least he was trying to control his temper—which he didn't always do.

But right now Harlan wouldn't have blamed Jonathan if he had exploded. The guy had pitched like a star for four innings. The Reds had gotten only one hit off him all that time.

And the Dodgers had been *slugging* the Reds' pitchers. Starting the bottom of the fifth, the score had been 11 to 0.

And then, *everything* had gone wrong. Coach Wilkens had decided that Anthony Ruiz, one of the team's two third graders, should learn to play first base.

But Anthony was a disaster.

He had dropped three throws—which all should have been outs—and the Reds had scored five runs.

And then, in the bottom of the sixth, with the score still safe at 11 to 5, he had made two more errors.

Jonathan, trying too hard for strikeouts, had also walked a guy, and then, with the bases loaded, had given up a hit.

And that's when Harlan had tagged a guy—without the ball.

Now the score was 11 to 8, and the Dodgers were in danger.

Only one runner was on—at second base—but the Dodgers still needed two outs. And outs had been hard to get lately.

Coach Wilkens walked to the mound. Harlan jogged out too.

"Jonathan, I know you're upset," the coach said. "But these younger boys have got to learn. Harlan will be the main catcher next year. And I'm thinking Anthony could be a first baseman."

Jonathan shook his head as if to say "You've got to be kidding."

"Well," the coach added, "I thought we'd be okay with that big lead."

Jonathan was a big, strong blond-haired boy, but right now he seemed to be using all his strength just to keep from popping off. Finally he said, in a controlled voice, "Don't you think we better get him off first for now—before we blow this game?"

"Well, no." The coach looked down. He had a quiet, soft way of speaking. "I want him to deal with the pressure. We can get those outs. Just relax and throw the way you were throwing earlier in the game. We'll be all right."

Jonathan nodded, but he didn't look happy.

Jonathan's father was using some control too. He was shouting for Jonathan to get the Reds out. But he hadn't yelled anything to the coach yet—and he hadn't screamed at Anthony.

That was progress.

"Harlan," the coach said, "that play at home could happen to any catcher. You just got anxious to get the tag down. Don't let it worry you. You're going to be a good catcher."

Harlan thanked the coach and trotted back to the plate.

Jonathan took some time. Harlan knew he was talking to himself, trying to get himself calmed down.

When he finally stepped to the rubber, he looked ready. He threw a good fastball on the outside part of the plate. The batter swung, and the ball squibbed off his bat down the first-base line.

It was rolling slowly, and Harlan chased after it.

Anthony charged it too.

They arrived at the same time, and both made a stab at the ball, but they only managed to knock each other's hand away.

When Harlan finally got hold of the ball, Jonathan was covering first. But it was too late. The runner was crossing the bag.

Harlan saw Jonathan shake his head and walk back to the mound. "Come *on,* let's get these guys!" was all that he said, but Harlan could hear how upset he was.

When the next batter hit a grounder to Ben Riddle at second, Harlan's heart almost stopped.

Ben was the other third grader, and he was not very sure of himself.

He didn't charge, but the ball came up for him. He caught it, but then he tried to throw too quickly and threw high.

Harlan muttered, "Oh no!" But Anthony jumped, and he did catch the ball. But Harlan could see that he had come down with both feet off the bag.

Harlan held his breath as Anthony stabbed at the bag with his foot.

Just in time!

"*OUT!*" the umpire hollered.

Harlan took a long sigh of relief.

Jonathan yelled, "Way to go, Ben! Way to go, Anthony!" He sounded as though he didn't quite believe that it had happened.

"Two away," the infielders all began to shout. They held up two fingers, like horns, to signal the outfielders that the Dodgers only needed one out.

But then Schulman, the Reds' catcher, slapped a little liner into center field, and another run scored.

The score was 11 to 9 now, and the tying runs were on base.

Harlan wondered if this game was ever going to end.

Jonathan was facing a rookie, a third grader who looked scared to death.

The only problem was that he was short as a tree stump and had almost no strike zone. He never swung the bat, and Jonathan tried too hard and found himself aiming the ball. He walked the kid.

Bases loaded. The winning run was on base.

Jonathan stood with his hands on his hips. Harlan knew he wanted a strikeout. Another substitute was coming up to bat—a taller kid, but not much of a hitter.

Jonathan fired a fastball that left the kid standing open-mouthed.

Harlan finally felt that things were going to turn out all right.

BAM! Another hard pitch. Strike two.

"You gotta swing if it's in there!" the Reds' coach was yelling.

But the pitch was in the dirt. It skipped under Harlan's glove, hit his shin guard, and bounced up the first-base line.

Harlan jerked his mask off and leaped after the ball. He saw the runner on third break for home.

This time Harlan made sure he had the ball before he went for the plate. But the runner was coming hard.

Harlan took one step and dove. He stretched his bare hand out with the ball—and felt the runner's shoe slam into his knuckles.

But that was okay.

He had tagged him in front of the plate. *"OOOOOUUUUUT!"*

Harlan took a deep breath, and for a moment he didn't get up. He lay in the dirt and enjoyed the feeling.

The game was finally over, and the Dodgers had hung on for the victory!

SECOND SEASON
BOX SCORE, GAME 7

Angel Park Dodgers 11

	ab	r	h	rbi
Jie 2b	2	1	1	0
White 3b	3	3	1	0
Sandoval ss	3	4	3	2
Swingle p	2	3	2	3
Malone cf	4	0	2	3
Roper 1b	2	0	1	2
Scott rf	4	0	2	1
Bacon c	2	0	0	0
Boschi lf	4	0	1	0
Riddle 2b	1	0	0	0
Sloan c	2	0	0	0
Ruiz 1b	1	0	0	0
ttl	30	11	13	11

Cactus Hills Reds 9

	ab	r	h	rbi
Trulis 2b	4	2	2	5
Gerstein 3b	3	1	2	1
Rutter p	3	0	0	0
Schulman c	3	0	2	3
Young lf	3	0	0	0
Bonthuis 1b	1	1	0	0
Lum ss	2	1	0	0
Harrison cf	2	2	1	0
Higdon rf	2	0	0	0
Hileman rf	0	1	0	0
Alfini lf	0	0	0	0
Charles 1b	0	1	0	0
	23	9	7	9

Dodgers 3 0 2 4 2 0—11
Reds   0 0 0 0 5 4—9

★ 2 ★

Footwork

After the game Coach Wilkens talked to Harlan.

"There's something I want you to know about Anthony," the coach told him. "But I don't want you to tell Anthony."

"Okay," Harlan said.

"I chose Anthony for the team because he needed to have some success. If he can learn the game, he's going to feel a lot better about himself. I guess that's a little project of mine."

Harlan had always suspected something like that, but he wondered whether there was any hope at all for Anthony.

"What I want you to do, Harlan—if you

don't mind—is to help him learn to play first base."

Harlan's mouth fell open. "Coach, I'm not that good at first myself. And now that I'm trying to learn to catch, I—"

"Harlan, I know all that. But if you could work out with him, you could teach him the footwork. He's left-handed and he's good-sized. It should be his best position."

"Yeah, but he has so much trouble catching the ball."

"I know. You had some trouble with that too, in the beginning. But he can learn. He's a smart boy. He may not ever be a star first baseman, but he can learn."

Harlan shrugged. "I'll try," Harlan said. But it was not something he was all that excited about.

"Harlan, as much as anything, he needs to believe he can do it."

"How do I teach him that?"

Coach Wilkens smiled. "I don't know. I'll leave that one up to you." And then he slapped Harlan on the back. "But something tells me you can do it."

That night Harlan thought about the things the coach had said. He talked to his parents, too. He decided the main thing Anthony needed was lots of practice.

The next day Harlan tried to teach Anthony some of the skills he needed: choosing a foot to anchor to the base; striding and reaching for the ball; watching the ball into his glove.

But things didn't go well.

Harlan soon felt like giving up the project as a lost cause.

Anthony was quiet. But Harlan soon wondered whether he was paying any attention. He seemed to forget everything Harlan told him—almost as soon as the words were out of Harlan's mouth.

And more than that, Harlan wondered whether Anthony really cared all that much.

Jacob Scott hit grounders to Kenny Sandoval, and Kenny fielded the ball and threw to Anthony. Jacob and Kenny had been rookies last year, but they hadn't been nearly as bad as Anthony. When Anthony did catch the ball, he usually forgot to keep his foot on the bag. Or sometimes he stepped on top of the bag, where he could get an ankle broken by a runner.

"I'm terrible," Anthony kept mumbling each time he made another mistake.

"Hey, I was lousy when I started," Harlan said. "It's not easy to learn. But you'll get it." Harlan not only remembered his own struggle to learn the position; he knew how much trouble he was having now, learning to be a catcher.

"Yeah," Jacob yelled to Anthony. "If Harlan can learn to play first, anyone can. You should have seen him last year. Our big pitcher, Bunson, kept threatening to kill him, he messed up so much."

"Really?" Anthony said, and he smiled a little.

"Yeah, really," Kenny said. He was walking over to Anthony. "You're lucky. Jonathan just tromps around on the mound and kicks dirt."

"He wanted to *kill me* yesterday," Anthony said.

"Yeah, well, we know all about that,"

Harlan told him. "We were all rookies last year. We not only had Bunson on our backs but a couple of other guys. I felt like quitting lots of times."

"That's what I feel like doing," Anthony said, and he looked down at the dirt.

"But don't," Harlan said. "If you stay at it, someday you'll be *GREAT*—like me." Harlan flexed his muscles as though he were a bodybuilder.

All the boys laughed, even Anthony.

"Let's practice some more," Jacob said.

And they did. Anthony even started to do a little better. Or at least he caught the ball more often, even if he messed up the footwork.

And the boys worked out again each day until Wednesday. At times Harlan thought Anthony was getting the idea.

But Harlan wondered about Anthony. The kid hardly ever laughed. He looked discouraged most of the time, or maybe even sad.

Anthony needed practice—but he needed more than that. Something seemed to be bothering him. And Harlan had no idea what it was.

Before the game on Wednesday, Harlan told Anthony not to worry. The game was with the A's—the worst team in the league. The Dodgers should have a big lead by the time Anthony got in the game.

And then the coach announced that Anthony would be a starter.

So would Harlan and Ben.

"This is a good night to give the younger players a chance to play a little more," Coach Wilkens said. "We're going to need them down the stretch."

No one complained, but Harlan knew everyone was remembering the near disaster of their last game. Harlan just hoped the coach wouldn't let things get out of hand before he brought in the experienced players.

But things started right.

The Dodgers were up first. Henry White singled to open the game, and Jacob walked.

Kenny, batting third, brought home Henry with another single.

Then big Jonathan hit a ball out of sight. *Home run!*

Suddenly the Dodgers were ahead 4 to 0.

Malone walked after that, and everyone was yelling to keep it going. But Eddie Boschi, Harlan, and Ben Riddle went out in order, and that ended the first inning.

Kenny was pitching, and he got off to a good start. He struck out the first two batters. The third batter flied out to left field.

One, two, three, and the Dodgers were back up again.

Of course, everyone knew that no real test had come yet. That came in the second inning, with the score still 4 to 0.

The cleanup batter, a stout kid who played catcher, hit a sharp grounder to Kenny. Kenny had lots of time, and he aimed a good throw at Anthony.

But Anthony stumbled as he tried to get his foot on the bag. He was on one knee when the throw came. He stuck up his glove and knocked the ball down. And then he grabbed it. But he wasn't touching the bag, and the runner blasted on by.

The A's really whooped it up, making fun of Anthony. At the same time all the Dodgers yelled to him that it was all right. But Harlan saw Anthony's head go down and his shoulders drop. He seemed to be expecting the worst.

And the worst came.

The next batter hit another grounder. Ben fielded the ball, and he should have gone to second for the force. But he got rattled and made a little looping throw to first.

If Anthony had stretched just right, he might have reached it. But he got the wrong foot on the bag, and the throw pulled him off.

Safe again.

Then Powell, the third baseman, socked a drive into left field that Eddie had to go almost to the foul line to field. Two runs scored, and Powell had himself a double.

The next batter, the right fielder, hit a

bouncer right at Anthony. And Anthony watched it right into his glove. . . .

And right out again!

The ball skipped on into right field and the runner scored.

Harlan felt sick. Poor Anthony looked as though he wanted to dig a hole and climb in.

And the A's wouldn't let up on him for a minute.

When the inning was over, and the score was tied, Harlan watched Anthony go straight to the coach. "Please take me out now," he said.

"Not yet, Anthony. You're getting the experience you need. And you're going to get better."

Harlan wondered.

★ 3 ★

Deep Trouble

The third inning went better. The Dodgers scored two runs and had a good rally going—until Ben and Anthony came up to bat. That ended the inning.

But at least the Dodgers were ahead again.

In the bottom of the inning Anthony made his first put-out. The play was routine—a ground ball and a good throw from Jonathan at shortstop.

But Anthony made it look hard. He pulled his foot off the bag before he caught the ball. Then he stumbled as he felt for the bag. But he touched the bag just in time.

The Dodgers gave Anthony a big cheer, and he looked relieved. Then the team got the other two batters without having to throw to first, and everyone ran to the dugout, shouting and cheering.

In fact, when the Dodgers' bats got hot in the top of the fourth, things began to look great.

Henry and Jacob both singled, and Kenny brought them home with a booming triple that barely stayed in the park. Then Jonathan drove Kenny home with a single.

With one out and the bases loaded—and three runs in—Ben and Anthony came up again. Harlan thought the coach might substitute for them now. But the coach yelled, "Come on, Ben. Knock these guys in."

Ben didn't.

He took a pretty good cut, but he hit a one-hopper straight back to the pitcher, and the pitcher tossed the ball home for the force.

That brought Anthony up with the bases

still loaded. Harlan could see how nervous the kid was. He didn't look like a player who wanted to blast one and make up for his errors in the field. Mostly he looked afraid that he would mess up again.

He let a ball go by and then got a called strike. But he made no move to swing the bat. Harlan figured he was hoping for a walk.

"Come on, Anthony," Harlan yelled. "Watch the ball. Just meet it."

But Anthony let another pitch go by.

Strike two.

"You gotta swing," Coach Wilkens yelled. "Stroke it."

Anthony listened, but when the pitch came, he took a weak, off-balanced swing.

Strike three. Anthony had killed another rally.

He turned away from the plate and walked slowly back to the dugout. He took a long look at Coach Wilkens.

Harlan knew exactly what he was hoping:

that he could be taken out of the game before he caused any more problems.

But Coach Wilkens called for Lian Jie to go into the game for Ben, and for Billy to go in at catcher.

Then he said, "Jenny, go in the game for Eddie in left field."

Anthony was still in the game. At first!

Harlan saw Anthony's disappointment. He stared at the coach as if to say "Why do you want to do this to me?"

But he walked slowly to first base. Harlan saw him take a long sweeping look across the bleachers. He seemed to be trying to spot someone.

Harlan looked to see who it might be, but he couldn't tell.

The score was 8 to 4 now, and Harlan hoped the inning would go easy on Anthony.

But no such luck.

Powell, the A's third baseman, went after the first pitch and socked a hard grounder at Henry. Henry made a good stop, but he had to make a long throw from third.

The throw came in a little low.

Anthony seemed to give up on himself. He stuck his glove down but didn't keep his eye on the ball. It skipped under his glove and rolled into foul territory.

Anthony hurried after the ball. But the runner was on second by the time Anthony picked it up.

Anthony walked back toward first and then on toward the mound. Harlan didn't know what he was doing.

Kenny turned to the umpire and called, "Time-out!" but Anthony handed Kenny the ball and kept right on walking toward the dugout. Coach Wilkens hurried out to meet him.

When the two met at the third-base line, Anthony looked down and said something. Harlan couldn't hear him, but he heard the coach say, "Yes, you can, Anthony. You can learn the position. It just takes time."

Anthony shook his head, but the coach said, "I can't take you out now anyway. I just put all the substitutes in." The coach patted him on the shoulder. "Son, don't worry. Just watch the ball into your glove. Concentrate. You can do it."

Anthony stood still for a few seconds, and then he turned and walked back across the diamond. All the A's players were laughing and making fun of him.

"Hey, fat-boy, who told you you could play first base?" one of the kids yelled.

His coach told him to be quiet, but it was too late to undo the damage. Poor Anthony looked as though he wanted to cry.

And things didn't get better.

The next batter struck out, but Sullivan, the left fielder, pounded a ground ball right at Anthony. Anthony knocked it down, but he had to grab the ball and get back to the bag. He just wasn't fast enough. The runner beat him to the bag.

Then the pitcher came up and socked a double that scored two runs.

The Dodgers were still ahead, but Harlan wondered how long they could hold the lead with most of the ground balls turning into hits.

But the next batter, Oshima, hit an easy grounder to Lian. Anthony caught the throw from Lian for the out, and Harlan dared to hope that Anthony's confidence might take a leap.

And maybe that's what would have happened.

But another disaster was coming.

The next batter bounced a high hopper toward Anthony. The ball came up just right, and Anthony gloved it.

He had it! All he had to do was take a couple of steps to the bag for the final out.

But the runner on third was streaking home. Anthony seemed not to understand that if he could make the out at first, the run wouldn't count at home. Instead of tagging first, he wound up and fired the ball to Billy.

But the throw was wild and bounced off the screen.

The run scored—which was bad enough—
but then everyone in the place seemed to
think they had to explain to Anthony how
stupid he had been.

Jonathan yelled from shortstop, "Anthony,
think!"

That was nice compared to the stuff the
A's were yelling.

"You idiot," a big voice rang out. "You
had the third out and you didn't take it!"

Harlan knew that Anthony felt like the
biggest idiot in the world. He stared straight
ahead while everyone yelled at him.

If only that had been the end of it.

But the center fielder was the next batter, and he calculated the Dodgers' weak-
ness. He pushed a bunt up the first-base line.
Kenny tried to get to it but couldn't.

Anthony hurried forward, took a clumsy
stab at the ball, and watched it roll right be-
tween his legs.

And then the next batter swung down on
the ball, purposely hitting a ground ball to
the right side.

Anthony let this one get through him again, and the ball rolled into right field.

Two runs scored and the Dodgers were *behind*. The A's were the worst team in the league, and they were ahead of the Dodgers!

★ 4 ★

Smart Play

By the time the fourth inning was over, the A's had six runs and were ahead 10 to 8.

The Dodgers came back to the dugout looking as though they had all taken a good beating.

"How can we let the stupid A's score ten runs?" Jonathan said, and he kicked the fence. "Why does the coach keep . . ."

He stopped. But everyone knew what he meant. Especially Anthony.

And Harlan was thinking the same thing: Anthony needed experience, but he was going to cost the Dodgers the game—plus any chance of winning the season's first-half championship.

All the same, the coach was yelling, "Come on, kids, let's score some runs and get that lead back."

And Harlan was sure they could do that. He shouted to Henry, "Knock the *cover* off the ball. Let's show these guys."

But Henry bounced a grounder to the shortstop and was out on a close play. Jacob, who had been on base every time until now, got under a ball and lifted it to short center field for an easy out. And then Kenny made a big mistake.

He hit a clean single, but he tried to use his speed to stretch it into a double.

The gamble backfired. The right fielder—who didn't have much of an arm—made a decent throw, and Kenny slid right into the tag.

Going to the bottom of the fifth, the Dodgers were still down by two.

At least things didn't get any worse. The

A's were substituting now, and some weak hitters came up in the bottom of the order. Kenny struck out the first two batters, and then he got the final out on a fly to left.

Anthony hadn't had to make a play, which was probably good, but he still hadn't had much of anything to feel proud of either. Harlan wished that something would go right for him.

And yet, Harlan was almost sure that wouldn't happen. Anthony sat on the bench with his head down. He had lost every ounce of belief in himself.

At least Jonathan was still convinced the Dodgers could come back. He waved his fist at his teammates and said, "All *right!* This is it. We gotta get the lead back. I'll start it off."

And that's what he did. He walked to the batter's box, took a couple of practice swings, and set himself. When the pitch came in, he took a sweet cut, snapped his wrists, and laced the ball to left field.

The ball got by the left fielder and went for a double.

Sterling Malone nodded when Jonathan yelled to him to bring him home, and then Sterling pounced on the first pitch. He drove the ball deep to left-center, over the fielder's head.

Jonathan scored, and Sterling rolled around second and on to third with a triple.

Jenny Roper hammered another hit, and just like that the Dodgers had tied the game.

"The A's are *nothing*," Billy Bacon told his teammates. "They're not worth the lint in my belly button. Let's show 'em what we can do. Let's keep scoring runs!"

He walked to the plate and shot a hard grounder at the shortstop. The shortstop fielded the ball but then threw high to second. The ball rolled into right field and everyone was safe.

The runners ended up on second and third.

Lian then chopped the ball on the ground to the right side. The ball was hit slowly, and the second baseman had no chance to cut off the run at home.

He threw Lian out, but the run scored, and now the Dodgers were on top again, 11 to 10.

But Anthony was up.

"Get a hit!" Coach Wilkens yelled to him. He clapped his hands and smiled. "You can do it."

And Anthony really tried.

He swung hard and sort of wildly, as though he didn't really expect to hit the ball. But at least he wasn't standing there waiting for a walk.

The result was still the same.

He struck out. And then he had to walk back to the dugout while the A's players made fun of him again.

Harlan waited until Anthony got back to the bench, and then he sat down next to him. "Anthony, we've worked on your fielding all week. But we need to work on your hitting, too. You gotta watch the ball all the way in."

Anthony shrugged as if to say "What good will it do?" Harlan didn't know what else to say to him.

At least Henry White came through. He whistled a line drive past the third baseman, and Billy scored.

Jacob had less luck. The shortstop caught his line drive. But the Dodgers were up by two again, and all they needed were three outs. If only they could avoid disaster this time.

As Harlan followed Anthony from the dugout, he heard the coach say, "Anthony, I just told Jenny to play first base in this last inning. So you play left field."

Harlan wondered. It was a gamble. Anthony hadn't shown any better skill at catching fly balls than he had at fielding grounders.

But first base usually got more action than

left field, and the coach had decided to go back to his experienced player.

The decision looked good when the first batter hit a slow grounder to shortstop and Jonathan had to hurry his throw. Jenny stretched and made the catch for a bang-bang out at first.

Harlan knew there was no way that Anthony would have made the play.

And then Kenny got a strikeout.

Harlan breathed a sigh of relief.

They only needed one more out.

Losing to the A's would have been the worst thing that could have happened. And now they only needed . . .

But things couldn't be that easy.

Smith, the catcher, hit a shot over the shortstop's head. Someone really fast—like Jenny—might have been able to charge the ball and catch it in the air.

But Anthony had no chance.

At least he didn't let the ball get by him. He held the runner to a single.

But then the pitcher blooped a lucky hit into right field, and the runner on first went all the way to third.

The tying runs were on base.

And that's when Powell lifted a fly ball to short left field.

Harlan's heart stopped. Anthony came in a couple of steps, but he looked unsure, as though he had maybe lost the ball in the high sky.

Jonathan was running out from shortstop as hard as he could. Harlan knew that he would make the catch if he possibly could—and not leave the ball to Anthony.

Anthony came in a little more, but he never really tried for the ball. He let Jonathan dive for it and . . . barely miss it.

He even let Jonathan scramble up and grab the ball and make the throw.

The runner from third scored. And the throw to second was going to be late.

Lian took the throw and then . . . or *NO!*

Suddenly he spun around and started chasing the ball. Harlan couldn't see the ball, but he knew it must have gotten by him.

The runner on second jumped up and headed for third. But that's when Lian abruptly turned and threw to third. He had had the ball all the time!

The runner was out by a mile.

Just like that, the game was over.

It took Harlan a few seconds to realize what had happened. Lian had faked the ball getting by him. The runner had fallen for the fake.

Everyone mobbed Lian. Harlan ran out and joined the celebration.

The Dodgers jumped on each other as though they had just beaten one of the really good teams. They knew they had avoided the big disaster. They were still alive for the championship.

Then Harlan remembered Anthony.

He looked around, but Anthony wasn't on the field, and he wasn't at the dugout.

And then Harlan spotted him. He had already crossed the park.

He was getting out of there as fast as he could.

Alone.

SECOND SEASON

BOX SCORE, GAME 8

Angel Park Dodgers 12   **Paseo A's 11**

	ab	r	h	rbi		ab	r	h	rbi
White 3b	4	2	2	0	Oshima 2b	4	0	1	1
Scott rf	3	2	2	0	Santos 1b	3	1	0	0
Sandoval p	4	2	3	3	De Klein cf	4	1	1	0
Swingle ss	4	3	4	4	Smith c	3	3	2	2
Malone cf	2	2	2	2	Chavez p	2	1	1	0
Boschi lf	3	0	1	0	Powell 3b	3	2	3	4
Sloan c	3	0	1	1	Reilly rf	1	1	0	0
Riddle 2b	3	0	0	0	Sullivan lf	0	1	0	0
Ruiz 1b	4	0	0	0	Naile p	2	1	1	2
Roper 1b	1	1	1	1	Henegan lf	1	0	0	0
Jie 2b	1	0	0	1	Trout rf	1	0	0	0
Bacon c	0	0	0	0	Watrous p	1	0	0	0
ttl	**32**	**12**	**16**	**12**		**25**	**11**	**9**	**9**

Dodgers 4 0 2 2 0 4—12
A's 0 4 0 6 0 1—11

Fastball

Coach Wilkens talked to the team after the game. "Listen, kids," he said, "I made a mistake today."

He was standing in front of them and they were all sitting on the grass. The sun was almost down, and the red sky made a silhouette of Coach Wilkens's slender body.

"I thought if I let Anthony play the whole game he'd get a hit or make a good catch—or something. I figured we could beat the A's, and Anthony would build some confidence."

"He was crying when he left," Eddie told the coach.

"I know he was. I'm going to go over to

his house right now. I'm afraid his confidence is in the sewer."

The coach looked at Harlan, who was at the back of the group. "Some of you boys have been working with him. Keep doing that, okay? And all of us have got to keep supporting him."

"Coach?" Jonathan said.

"Yeah."

"I don't mean to sound . . . mean, or anything. But maybe he'd be better off if he got into some other sport."

"Well, Jonathan, that might be true. Or maybe I should have let him play in the minor league this year. But I still think he can play. He's got *much* more ability than he's shown so far."

Harlan hoped that was true. He felt sorry for Anthony.

So did Kenny and Jacob.

The three of them rode home on their bikes together. Along the way they talked things over and decided they would work with Anthony even more and make sure something went right for him.

That night Harlan called Anthony. His mother answered the phone.

"I'm sorry, but he already went to bed," she told Harlan.

"Oh. Well, tell him we're going to practice tomorrow, after school."

"Is this Harlan?"

"Yeah."

"The coach came over, but Anthony told him he didn't want to play anymore. He finally said he'd think about it some more, but he told me, after, that he was quitting."

"I'll talk to him, Mrs. Ruiz. I don't think he should quit."

"Well, I don't either, but—well—there's something Anthony probably hasn't told you."

Harlan waited.

"Anthony's father moved out last Sunday. We're getting a divorce. It's very hard for Anthony. Baseball should be fun, but right now it's just one more problem for him."

Harlan didn't know what to say.

"I still think it's better for him to be with

you boys, and with the coach. I want him to play. But I'm not going to tell him he *has* to."

"Yeah, I can see what you mean," Harlan said. "Maybe I can talk to him about it tomorrow."

"Yes. I think that might be good."

When Harlan put the phone down, he thought he understood a lot better. He could see why Anthony had seemed in another world at times.

And later that night, as Harlan lay in bed, he remembered Anthony walking out to first base and then looking at the stands, as though he were hoping to see someone.

Maybe he had wanted to see his parents there.

On Thursday when classes were over, Harlan waited for Anthony outside the school. But as soon as Anthony saw Harlan he said, "I'm not playing anymore. I decided to quit."

"I thought you were thinking it over."

"I did. I'm quitting."

"Anthony, don't quit yet. Some things just take a while to learn."

"I won't ever be good at baseball," Anthony said. He started to walk away.

"Anthony, your mom told me about your dad, and I know that must be—"

"I don't want to talk about that."

Harlan hurried to catch up. "Hey, man," he said, laughing, "you'll miss us if you're not practicing with us every day."

Anthony didn't answer, but he slowed up a little, as though he knew there was something to that.

"How about trying for one more week? Two games? Kenny and Jacob and I will work with you every day."

"No . . . I don't think so."

But Harlan heard some wavering in Anthony's voice. And it wasn't long until he had Anthony agreeing to meet him at the park in an hour.

And that night the four players—plus Lian and Henry—worked for a long time on fielding, footwork at first base, and hitting.

There were times when Anthony really

started to show signs of improvement. And then it would all be gone again. He just couldn't keep his mind on baseball.

When Saturday came, Anthony seemed content to start out the game on the bench. The game was with the Padres, who were getting better all the time.

Harlan wanted to see Anthony do well, but he was also worried about the game. It was another *must-win* game, and Harlan hated to think what Anthony could do to it—or how he would feel if he really messed up.

Things started well for the Dodgers, though. The Padres were up first, but Jonathan was pitching and he was *smoking* the ball.

Lundberg, the second baseman, watched two strikes *smack* Billy's glove, and then he finally decided he'd better swing. Jonathan changed up, and poor Lundberg swung before the ball was halfway to the plate.

"Yer outta there!" the young umpire hollered, and Lundberg gave him an angry glance as he walked back to the dugout.

Jorgensen, the girl who played left field,

did no better, except she did foul off one pitch.

And then "Bad News" Roberts came up. He was a cocky kid. He knocked the dirt from his shoes and adjusted his batting gloves before he stepped to the plate.

But the kid was more than a show-off. He was a natural hitter. Jonathan had to put something extra on the ball.

Roberts took a healthy cut at Jonathan's first pitch and saw nothing but dust as the ball *banged* into Billy's glove.

He took another fastball for a ball outside. Then he seemed to guess that Jonathan might go to his change-up.

But he guessed wrong.

He was still standing there when the ball smacked the glove.

Bad News didn't like that. "Try that pitch again," he yelled to Jonathan. "I'll knock it out of here."

Jonathan nodded, and then he fired a wicked fastball, in on Roberts's hands. Bad News swung with everything he had and snapped the bat right in half.

The ball trickled out in front of the plate,

and Billy threw Roberts out. But as Bad News ran back to the dugout, he yelled to Jonathan, "Just wait until *you* get up!"

Harlan knew what that meant. Bad News was pitching. Harlan just hoped the Dodgers could score some runs off the guy.

In the bottom of the inning, when Lian could only muster a weak grounder and Henry struck out, the chances didn't look very good.

But Kenny let a couple of pitches go by and then met the next pitch on the nose. The ball shot off his bat on a line and just kept carrying to left field.

Harlan thought it would be an easy catch for the left fielder, but the ball was really tagged. It carried and carried, and . . . *cleared the fence!*

The Dodgers had themselves a run.

And Bad News was mad.

When Jonathan stepped up to bat, Roberts was waiting.

He threw a *blazer*—way inside.

Jonathan spun away and hit the dirt, and he came up fighting mad. He took a couple of quick steps toward the mound.

But Coach Wilkens yelled, "No, Jonathan!" and Jonathan stopped.

And then the coach trotted to home plate. Harlan heard him say, "Ump, there's no question in my mind that the pitcher threw a pitch at my player—on purpose. Let's get it stopped before someone gets hurt."

The umpire walked out and talked to Roberts, but as he walked back, Harlan could see that Bad News had a little smirk on his face.

It was going to be some game.

★ 6 ★

Good News, Bad News

Bad News didn't throw close to Jonathan again, but he threw nothing but *heat*.

Jonathan hung tough. He fouled off a couple of pitches, and he let some go by, and then, finally, he lost the battle.

He struck out on a pitch that was probably ball four.

From that point the game turned into a pitchers' duel. Each team managed a couple of hits, but no one scored.

Harlan and Anthony entered the game in the bottom of the fourth—and both struck out. But then, they weren't alone.

After four innings the score was still 1 to 0.

Coach Wilkens had Ben play second, and he put Harlan at first base. He sent Anthony out to play right field for Jacob.

Harlan knew that the coach was trying to take some pressure off Anthony, and he also knew that the team had a much better chance of winning if Anthony stayed away from first base.

Now the test would begin. Ben and Anthony would have to come through. Harlan would too. Harlan was better at first base than he was at catcher—but he knew he wasn't as good as Jenny.

The first batter in the fifth inning was a small boy, a third grader, who batted for the third baseman. He was hopeless against Jonathan's fastball. He struck out.

But Joey Palmer, the shortstop, bounced a high hopper to third base. Henry waited for the ball to come down and then *gunned* it to first.

But he was a split second late. Palmer was on.

The next batter, another rookie, got his

bat out late but managed to scoot a ground ball toward Ben at second.

If Lian had been playing, he would have tried for the double play. But Ben gloved the ball and took the sure out at first.

Not bad, really. Ben was getting better all the time.

And then Jonathan racked up another strikeout on another sub, and the Dodgers were out of the inning.

Things had gone well. Anthony hadn't been tested, but that meant he hadn't done anything wrong. And Ben had made a good play.

In the bottom of the inning Billy bounced a ball at the new third baseman—the rookie—and the kid dropped the ball.

Eddie and Ben both struck out, but then Henry snapped a drive into center field. With two outs Billy was on the go, and he motored around to third.

Then Kenny hit another hard smash, but this one stayed in the park, and Jorgensen went back and made the catch.

Bad News seemed to be weakening a little—but too late. The big thing now was for the Dodgers to get three more outs and make their one-run lead hold up.

But that wouldn't be easy. The top of the order was coming up, and Jonathan had been throwing hard for five innings.

When Lundberg stepped up to the plate, his teammates, and all the Padres' fans, really picked up the noise. The Padres had to come through *right now* and they knew it.

Jonathan threw a flaming fastball. Lundberg swung late and missed. He stepped out of the box and banged his bat on the ground.

"Come on, Cory," Bad News yelled. "You gotta do it. You can hit a *fifth grader.*"

Lundberg nodded and stepped back to the plate.

Jonathan came with his curve. But the pitch was up, and Lundberg wasn't fooled. He drove the ball past Jonathan's head into center field.

The Padres' players went crazy. Roberts

came out to the on-deck area. "You're in trouble, *Swat*," he yelled to Jonathan. "Watch who does the *swatting* now."

Harlan felt the butterflies in his stomach. He looked around at Anthony. The guy was standing stiff as a statue. Harlan knew how scared he was.

But then Harlan noticed something else. Anthony wasn't looking toward home plate. He was staring out toward the parking lot. That was the second time Harlan had seen him doing that. He wondered if Anthony was looking for his parents.

But Harlan had no time to give the question much thought.

Jorgensen hit a hard grounder that was heading past Kenny. Kenny darted to his left, dove, and . . . *speared* the ball.

He had no chance to make the play at first. But Kenny scrambled to his knees and flipped the ball to Ben, who made a nice catch—just in time.

The Dodgers gave Kenny—and Ben—a big cheer.

They needed two more outs.

But Roberts was coming up—and he looked ready to *kill* the ball. He skipped all his show-off stuff and stepped into the box. He swung the bat only once and came set.

He was coiled like a spring.

Jonathan stared in at Billy, took the sign, and nodded, and then blasted a fastball past Roberts.

Roberts fumed. "C'mon, ump, the ball was outside!" he barked.

But he got set again. And when the pitch came in, he almost jumped he swung so hard.

And he *connected*.

The ball zipped past third base before Henry could move.

Eddie ran hard and reached the ball in the corner. He spun and made a great throw. Roberts had a double, but Jorgensen had had to stop at third.

The Dodgers hadn't lost the lead yet. But the tying and winning runs were in scoring position with only one out.

Harlan could hear his heart beating in his

ears, feel it in his chest. Somehow, the Dodgers had to get those two outs.

Brenchley, the catcher, was coming up, and Roberts, on second base, was all over Jonathan.

But Jonathan didn't look back. He fired two fastballs for strikes and then threw a curve that was outside. Brenchley took a big sucker swing—*SWISH!*—and missed everything.

Two outs.

"All right!" Harlan shouted. And all the Dodgers yelled to Jonathan to get the final out.

Durkin, the first baseman, was up next. His hitting had improved a lot this year.

This time Jonathan came with a fastball outside, and Durkin started to swing and held up. But he swung at the next pitch and lifted an easy fly to the right side.

Harlan was thrilled for an instant, and then he looked back and saw Anthony standing, staring into the air. He didn't seem to have the ball spotted.

Harlan took off and so did Ben, and finally Anthony came rumbling forward. But it was too late.

The ball dropped on the grass and the run scored.

Harlan got to the ball first. He grabbed it with his bare hand, twisted around, and fired the ball home.

Roberts was coming hard, but Harlan threw a strike!

Bad News was out by three steps.

But the game was tied.

The Dodgers would have to come through in the bottom of the sixth or face extra innings.

The Dodgers ran to the dugout, and they yelled to each other that they could still win the game. But Harlan knew they were upset with Anthony.

No one said a word to him, but Harlan heard Billy whisper to Jonathan, "We should have let him quit. He doesn't *want* to play."

And Jonathan said, "What was he doing? He acted like he wasn't even watching when the guy hit the ball."

Harlan wondered if that wasn't right. But he didn't know what else he could do.

The best news was that *Swat* was up. And he wanted the win bad. Pitchers were allowed only six innings. If he couldn't end the game now, new pitchers would take over in the seventh.

Jonathan stepped to the plate and cocked his bat. Brenchley, the skinny catcher, yelled to Roberts, "Hey, Bad News, this is an easy out!"

Roberts laughed. But not for long.

He threw a hard fastball, and Jonathan was *ready*.

He *stroked* it!

There was never any question.

The ball arched *way* over the left field fence.

Jorgensen looked up and watched it go. And then she slammed her glove on the grass.

Bad News kicked dirt all over the infield as Jonathan trotted around the bases.

But the Dodgers were going crazy. They

were all waiting for Swat as he headed home.

All except Anthony.

Anthony was still sitting on the bench. He was leaning over, staring into the dirt at his feet.

SECOND SEASON

BOX SCORE, GAME 9

Santa Rita Padres　1 　　　Angel Park Dodgers　2

	ab	r	h	rbi		ab	r	h	rbi
Lundberg 2b	3	0	1	0	Jie 2b	2	0	1	0
Jorgensen lf	3	1	0	0	White 3b	3	0	1	0
Roberts p	3	0	2	0	Sandoval ss	3	1	1	1
Brenchley c	3	0	0	0	Swingle p	2	1	1	1
Durkin 1b	3	0	2	1	Malone cf	2	0	1	0
Blough 3b	1	0	0	0	Roper 1b	1	0	0	0
Palmer ss	2	0	1	0	Scott rf	1	0	0	0
Campbell cf	1	0	0	0	Bacon c	1	0	0	0
Valenciano rf	1	0	0	0	Boschi lf	2	0	0	0
Nakatani 3b	1	0	0	0	Sloan c	1	0	0	0
Orosco cf	1	0	0	0	Ruiz rf	1	0	0	0
Rollins rf	1	0	0	0	Riddle 2b	1	0	0	0
ttl	**23**	**1**	**6**	**1**		**20**	**2**	**5**	**2**

Padres　　0 0 0　0 0 1—1
Dodgers　1 0 0　0 0 1—2

★ 7 ★

Giant Game

After the game all the Dodgers stuck around to watch the Giants play.

The Dodgers still had a chance for the first-half championship, but the hope was thin.

The Giants had to lose to the A's. The Dodgers would play the Giants on Wednesday, and maybe they could beat them, but the Dodgers had two losses. The Giants had none.

After a couple of innings, when the Giants were already ahead 10 to 0, the Dodgers all knew that their hopes had gone down the drain. Most of the players left.

Harlan felt bad about the Giants winning the first half, but he felt the team was coming together now. He felt confident the Dodgers could take the second half and still win the season championship.

But he had something else on his mind besides. He told Kenny and Jacob, "I wish we could do something to help Anthony."

The boys had a talk about that, but they didn't know what they could do. They would keep practicing with him—and be his friend—but they couldn't change what was happening in his home.

At practices, Harlan went out of his way to talk to Anthony, and he kept showing him all he could about playing first base. Sometimes Anthony seemed to be getting the idea, but he would always slip back into that quiet mood.

And then he would lose his concentration and do everything all wrong again.

On Wednesday when game time came, the Dodgers didn't look very excited. The coach called them together and talked to them. "Okay, kids," he said, "I know you think we have nothing to win, but we do."

For a moment Harlan thought maybe the Giants had lost after all.

"We can't win the first-half championship now," the coach told them. "But we need to show the Giants we're a better team than we were early in the season. We need to send them into the second half knowing they can lose."

Jonathan was sitting behind Harlan. Harlan heard him whisper to Billy, "If we didn't have to let Anthony play, we might have a chance."

And Billy mumbled, "I know. He's killing us."

Harlan knew that was true in a way, but he also knew that part of Anthony's problem was that the other players were *expecting* him to mess up.

The coach had one more thing to add. "The Giants are showing some class this year.

Let's do the same. Let's be good sports, and let's support each other. And let's *beat* those guys!"

The players cheered and jumped up. And then they ran to the dugout. They were batting first, and they were determined to get off to a good start.

Harlan wasn't starting, but he was excited. He knew it was time for the team to prove to itself what it could do. The coach was right. This game was very big in some ways.

Harlan also knew that Anthony had to turn things around soon—probably today—or he never would. In fact, if things kept going the way they had, he was pretty sure Anthony would quit.

And one thing was sure. Anthony's confidence hadn't improved at all. Harlan watched him sit down on the bench. He didn't look at anyone. In fact, he stared at the ground in front of his own feet.

But the rest of the team was *psyched.*

"Get on base, Lian!" Sterling yelled. "Let's whup these guys."

Lian always looked sure of himself. "We can hit House," he said. "Wait for his curve ball. It's slow."

"House" Hausberg was pitching for the Giants. And he looked *big* as a house. Still, it was not his fastball but his curve—no matter how slow it was—that was so tricky to hit.

Lian knew how to hit it. He let a fastball go by, and then he waited on the curve and just poked it into right field.

The Dodgers all jumped up. "Today we *do it!*" Henry yelled, and everyone cheered.

Jacob said, in his announcer's voice, "Something tells me the Dodgers are going to cut these Giants down to size today."

"Yes, Frank," he said, in his cowboy announcer's voice, "they just might make *midgets* out of them!"

The other players liked that.

Harlan noticed that the Giants were talking it up around the infield, but they didn't seem worried. Maybe they were a little too sure of themselves—a little too cocky after wrapping up the first-half title.

And then Harlan jumped straight in the air when he heard the *BOING* of a metal bat and saw Henry's line drive settle in for another single.

Kenny was coming up, and the Dodgers were all shouting to him to bring the runners home.

Kenny looked ready to do that.

And suddenly Hausberg couldn't get the ball—especially his curve—over the plate. Kenny never saw a pitch he could swing at. He walked on four pitches.

And now Jonathan was coming up.

There was no room for him on base. The House would have to throw strikes.

With the curve not working, Harlan knew that Hausberg would have to come with his fastball.

And Jonathan knew that too.

The first pitch was down the middle and Jonathan *smashed* it. If he had gotten it higher in the air, it would have landed in some other country. But it screamed past the left fielder, hit the fence on one bounce, and dropped straight down.

Runners were flying around the bases. By the time the fielder could make the long throw, Jonathan was slowing up to stop at third with a stand-up triple.

And then Sterling socked a hard liner of his own, and Swat trotted home with the fourth run.

It was 4–zip and still no outs.

When Jenny hit a sharp grounder through the hole for another single, the rally was still rolling.

Jacob lashed a drive that seemed to be heading for right field. But the big first baseman, a kid named Glenn, leaped in the air and stabbed the ball.

Jenny had taken a step off base, and Glenn came down and swiped his glove across her shoulder just before she could reach back and touch the base.

Double play!

After that, Hausberg settled down. He got his curve working and struck out Eddie for the third out.

All the same, the Dodgers had themselves four runs. They were in control.

And Kenny was looking very sharp on the mound. He put down the Giants in order in the first inning. He gave up one hit in the second and one in the third. And no runs.

But Hausberg was in the groove now too. And he got the Dodgers out with no problems in the second and third.

Then the top of the fourth came, and Coach Wilkens sent Anthony in to bat for Jacob.

Anthony walked slowly to the plate. He held the bat on his shoulder and watched the pitches go by.

But he never swung.

House had to throw five pitches to get three called strikes, but Anthony never even gave it a shot.

He turned and walked back to the dugout. And when he got there, Jonathan finally lost his temper.

"You're not even *trying!*" he yelled at Anthony. "You don't even *care*. Why don't you just quit the team, like you said you were going to. Then maybe *we'd* have a chance."

"Okay," Anthony said, and he walked to the end of the bench and sat down.

Harlan didn't know what to do.

★ 8 ★

Just in Time

Jonathan didn't have much time to think about Anthony.

Eddie hit a grounder that should have been an out, but Dave Weight, the Giants' usually sure-handed third baseman, booted the ball, and Eddie was on. It was a break the Dodgers could build on.

Billy was up next. He looked back at the dugout and said, "*Out*house can't get me out. I can *smell* his curve ball."

But Billy hit a slow roller that got him thrown out. At least he moved the runner to second, and now if Lian could get a hit, the Dodgers could pick up another run.

And then the coach put Ben in for Lian.

The Dodgers yelled to Ben that he could do it. Still, Harlan could tell that no one expected much.

But Ben showed them. He drilled a shot back up the middle for a clean single.

RBI!

The Dodgers all went wild. They yelled to Ben that he was going to be a star. And Ben grinned as though he had just won the final game of the World Series.

Ben was on the team!

That was great, but Harlan thought of Anthony. He was still sitting at the end of the bench with his head down.

When Henry flied out, the Dodgers headed back to the field with a five-run lead. Things looked good.

Then the surprise came.

The coach sent Harlan in to catch for Billy, moved Jenny to right, and had Anthony play first base.

A five-run lead was great, but it could disappear fast if Anthony started messing up.

And yet, Harlan knew what the coach was

up to. Somehow, this team had to win with their rookies doing the job, or they never would be a team that could go all the way.

Harlan got his catcher's gear on, but he knew what he had to do. He ran to first base, not the plate.

"Anthony," he called. "I need to talk to you."

Anthony looked at him with those soft, sad eyes, and Harlan could see that he was already expecting the worst.

"Listen, Anthony, you can do it. You've practiced a lot, and you're getting better every day. But you gotta *try*."

Anthony's head shot up. Harlan knew immediately that he had said the wrong thing. His words were almost the same ones Jonathan had used. "I *am* trying," Anthony said.

"Anthony, listen to me. I know you feel bad about your dad and everything, but you gotta—"

"Shut up, Harlan," Anthony said. He turned and walked away.

The umpire was shouting to Harlan to get

himself behind the plate. There was nothing he could do now. But he could sense that trouble was ahead.

And it didn't take long to start. Glenn, the tall first baseman, started off the inning with a sharp grounder right at Anthony. Anthony backed up and let the ball play him, and it hit him square in the chest. He ran after it, but he couldn't get to it fast enough. Glenn was on.

Harlan yelled to Anthony not to worry, but he saw that defeated look in his eyes.

The next batter hit the ball on the ground to the left side, and Jonathan scooped it up and played the force at second.

Ben was a little awkward in taking the throw and he juggled it for a second. But he got the ball under control just in time for the out.

Then Hausberg rolled a slow grounder up the line toward third. Henry had to charge and throw in a hurry.

The throw would have made any first baseman stretch, but Anthony got his feet tangled. He was off balance as he reached

for the ball. He almost fell down, and the
ball caromed off his glove.

The runner went all the way to third, and
Hausberg thundered on to second.

The next batter, the center fielder, timed
one of Kenny's good fastballs and banged
the ball into the gap in right-center for a
double.

The score was suddenly 5 to 2, and there
was only one out.

And all the Dodgers knew the truth. If
Jenny had been on first, there would be two
outs, maybe three. And no runs.

But that was not the worst part. The coach
had to let Anthony play for six outs—that
was the rule—and five more outs with him
on first base would not be easy.

And then Harlan saw something change.

Anthony was looking up to the bleachers,
and he suddenly looked different. He didn't
look exactly happy. But he looked alive
again.

He got ready at first, and he took an in-
fielder's position—as though he meant
business for a change.

Kenny threw a good fastball for a strike, and Harlan threw the ball back, and then he glanced at Anthony again.

"Come on, let's get this guy," Anthony yelled to Harlan. His voice sounded sort of shaky—scared. But at least he was yelling.

And then, just as Kenny was getting ready to pitch again, Harlan heard a man yell, "Come on, Anthony. Let's get these guys out."

Harlan didn't know the voice.

But he knew who it must be.

The batter didn't get good wood. He hit a come-back grounder to Kenny. Kenny spun and looked the runner back to second, and then he made the short throw to first. He didn't burn the ball, and the throw was right at Anthony's chest.

Any kid in the world could have caught it.

It was no big deal.

But Anthony caught this one, and Harlan knew it *did* mean something.

"Way to go!" his dad was yelling—for the first time all year.

All the Dodgers yelled to Anthony that he had done a good job. Anthony just walked back to his position and got ready for the next play. But Harlan could see the change in his eyes.

The next batter hit a routine fly ball to Jenny, and the inning was over.

The Dodgers still had a three-run lead, and they now had half of those six outs.

But something more than that had happened. The Dodgers seemed excited when they came back to the dugout. They all told each other they were going to get some more runs, and Harlan could tell they believed it.

Kenny started with a blooper that dropped in for a single, and then Jonathan laced a hard-shot single to left. Malone followed with a bomb that hit the fence in left-center.

Two runs scored and Sterling had himself a double.

Jenny was up next, and Anthony was going out to the on-deck circle.

"Let's keep it going," Harlan said to Anthony. He slapped him on the back.

Anthony didn't say anything, but he

looked more determined than he had all year.

When Jenny slashed a single to right, another run scored, and the Dodgers were having fun. If they could handle the Giants, they knew they could beat any team in the league!

"Look out for the Dodgers in the second half!" Billy yelled. "We're on a roll now!"

As Anthony strode to the plate, the Dodgers cheered. And up in the stands, a voice that kept getting louder was shouting, "Get a hit, Anthony. You can do it!"

Anthony swung hard at the first pitch. And missed.

"Anthony!" Harlan yelled. Anthony stepped out of the box and looked around. "Remember. Just meet the ball. Watch it all the way to your bat."

Anthony nodded and stepped back into the box. The next pitch was outside, but Harlan saw how he had followed the ball. He knew something good was about to happen.

And then big Anthony met the next pitch. *Square.*

Solid.

The ball jumped off his bat and darted into center field.

For a moment Anthony forgot to run. He just watched the ball. But when he finally took off, he gave it everything. He *thundered* his way to first, and then he spun around and shot his fists into the air.

"I did it!" he yelled.

But he was not looking at his teammates. He was looking up to the stands, where a big man was standing with his own fists still in the air.

"Way to go, son. Way to go!" he kept yelling.

The Dodgers kept rolling after that. They scored another run in the fifth and two more in the sixth.

And they shut the Giants down.

Anthony played first for nine outs, not six, and he made three more put-outs—one on a pretty good stretch.

When the game was all over and the Dodgers had slapped hands with the Giants, the big man who'd been cheering for Anthony came down and gave his boy a big hug. Harlan heard him say, "Anthony, I'm sorry I've missed your games. I talked to your mom, and she said you haven't been very happy with me. I guess I've been thinking too much about my own problems. I'm sorry. I'll try to make it to every game from now on. Is that okay? Are we buddies again?"

"Sure," Anthony said, nodding and looking like a whole new kid. All he had needed was his dad's support—or that was a lot of what he needed.

But before he left, Anthony came to Harlan and told him thanks.

"What for?" Harlan asked.

"For helping me. And talking me into staying on the team."

"Hey, we need you," Harlan said. "You're going to help us win the championship."

"I don't know. I'm still not very good," Anthony said.

But he was smiling, and Harlan knew he was starting to believe he could play the game.

SECOND SEASON

BOX SCORE, GAME 10

Angel Park Dodgers 11

	ab	r	h	rbi
Jie 2b	2	1	1	0
White 3b	4	1	1	0
Sandoval p	3	3	3	0
Swingle ss	4	3	3	4
Malone cf	4	1	2	3
Roper 1b	4	1	3	2
Scott rf	1	0	0	0
Boschi lf	3	1	0	0
Bacon c	2	0	0	0
Ruiz lb	3	0	1	0
Riddle 2b	2	0	1	1
Sloan c	1	0	1	1
ttl	**33**	**11**	**16**	**11**

Blue Springs Giants 2

	ab	r	h	rbi
Nugent lf	1	0	0	0
Sanchez ss	2	0	0	0
Weight 3b	3	0	1	0
Glenn 1b	2	0	1	0
Cooper 2b	3	1	0	0
Hausberg p	2	1	0	0
Spinner cf	2	0	1	2
Waganheim rf	1	0	0	0
Dodero c	2	0	1	0
Zonn rf	2	0	0	0
Villareal lf	1	0	0	0
Stevens cf	1	0	0	0
	22	**2**	**4**	**2**

Dodgers 4 0 0 1 4 2—11
Giants 0 0 0 2 0 0—2

SECOND SEASON

League standings after ten games:

Giants	9–1
Dodgers	8–2
Reds	5–5
Padres	4–6
Mariners	3–7
A's	0–10

Seventh game scores:

Dodgers	11	Reds	9
Giants	10	Mariners	2
Padres	7	A's	4

Eighth game scores:

Dodgers	12	A's	11
Giants	12	Reds	3
Mariners	3	Padres	2

Ninth game scores:

Dodgers	2	Padres	1
Giants	19	A's	2
Reds	12	Mariners	10

Tenth game scores:

Dodgers	11	Giants	2
Reds	4	Padres	1
Mariners	8	A's	6

SECOND-YEAR STATISTICS

JONATHAN SWINGLE

At-bats	Runs	Hits	RBIs	Avg.
30	14	22	23	.733

KENNY SANDOVAL

At-bats	Runs	Hits	RBIs	Avg.
33	17	20	15	.606

SECOND-YEAR STATISTICS

JENNY ROPER

At-bats	Runs	Hits	RBIs	Avg.
26	7	14	11	.538

SECOND-YEAR STATISTICS

JACOB SCOTT

At-bats	Runs	Hits	RBIs	Avg.
27	8	13	9	.481

STERLING MALONE

At-bats	Runs	Hits	RBIs	Avg.
29	7	13	11	.448

SECOND-YEAR STATISTICS

LIAN JIE

At-bats	Runs	Hits	RBIs	Avg.
27	7	12	6	.444

HENRY WHITE

At-bats	Runs	Hits	RBIs	Avg.
35	13	14	1	.400

SECOND-YEAR STATISTICS

HARLAN SLOAN

At-bats	Runs	Hits	RBIs	Avg.
14	3	5	3	.357

EDDIE BOSCHI

At-bats	Runs	Hits	RBIs	Avg.
27	6	7	1	.259

SECOND-YEAR STATISTICS

BILLY BACON

At-bats	Runs	Hits	RBIs	Avg.
13	4	2	3	.154

BEN RIDDLE

At-bats	Runs	Hits	RBIs	Avg.
15	1	2	1	.133

SECOND-YEAR STATISTICS

ANTHONY RUIZ

At-bats	Runs	Hits	RBIs	Avg.
9	0	1	0	.111

ALL-STAR OF THE MONTH

EDDIE
BOSCHI

Eddie is not the best player on the Angel Park Dodgers, but he's without a doubt the most improved. He has worked very hard to learn his position and improve his hitting skills. When he started Little League, kids called him "the stork" because he was so skinny, and he seemed all arms and legs. And the truth is, he was a very awkward player. But now he's a solid left fielder, a pretty fair pitcher, and not a bad hitter. He's come through in important situations for the Dodgers, and he gives every game his complete effort.

School has been much the same story for Eddie. He got off to a bad start in first grade. Reading was difficult for him. Arithmetic was easier, but he never had much confidence in himself. But he worked hard, and his reading kept improving. His parents spent a lot of time working on reading and spelling skills with him. His dad told him that sports were great but that school was much more important. If Eddie wanted to play baseball and basketball, he had to keep up with his schoolwork. That was just the push Eddie needed. He didn't want to lose his chance to play, so he made sure he did his very best work in school.

Eddie has some favorite television shows, and he likes to play Nintendo, but more than anything, he likes to spend time with friends. Eddie seems to know *everyone* in Angel Park. And he takes the time to talk to everyone he sees—from adults to little kids to neighborhood dogs. He drives his parents nuts with all his phone calls—and with so many friends coming around the house—but he's a fun kid, and they're glad that so many people like him.

What Eddie gives the Dodgers is that friendly spirit that every team needs. Eddie talks to every player, makes everyone feel part of the team, and has fun playing. When a teammate gets a little too uptight or begins to criticize one of the young players, Eddie always tries to keep the team together and feeling good about one another. And yet, he never talks about "team spirit." He just shows the players how to be good friends.

Eddie's parents grew up in Colorado, and they are avid skiers. So every Christmas the Boschis drive to "Grandma's house" in Boulder, and they spend almost every day on the slopes. Eddie may be the funniest-looking skier on the mountain, but he gets down and always seems to stay on his skis. His little sister is a much better skier than Eddie, but he doesn't care. He just enjoys the good ride and doesn't worry what anyone else thinks of his "style."

And maybe that's one way he helps the Dodgers. He doesn't have the talent that some of the other players have, but he gets the job done. The players who have more speed, more strength, more coordination, look at Eddie and know that he is getting the very most out of what he has. And they feel that they should do the same. They know he's someone they can depend on. He may not blast the big homers or throw a no-hitter, but he never lets them down either. No team can be made up entirely of super-heroes. Some players must be the dependable ones who play hard, have fun, and are always there, giving all they've got. And that's Eddie!

DEAN HUGHES has written many books for children, including the popular *Nutty* stories and *Jelly's Circus*. He has also published such works of literary fiction for young adults as the highly acclaimed *Family Pose*. Writing keeps Mr. Hughes very busy, but he does find time to run and play golf—and he loves to watch almost all sports. His home is in Utah. He and his wife have three children, all in college.

READ THESE OTHER ANGEL

#1 MAKING THE TEAM

Kenny, Harlan, and Jacob have officially made the team, but some of the older players—mostly team bully Rodney Bunson—seem bent on making life miserable for the three rookies. Can the third-grade Little Leaguers stand up to some big-league bullying?

#2 BIG BASE HIT

Awkward and big for his age, Harlan seems to do everything wrong—and it's making him wonder whether he really belongs on the team at all. But then the pitcher throws the ball, and Harlan gives the team just what they've all been waiting for: a big base hit!

#3 WINNING STREAK

Kenny's in a slump—and it spells big trouble for the undefeated Angel Park Dodgers. Jacob's got a few tricks that he thinks will help, but his wacky ideas only seem to make matters worse. Then he hits on the one trick that puts Kenny back in action, just in time to put the team back on a winning streak!

#4 WHAT A CATCH!

Brian desperately wants to make his last season in Little League his best ever, but his mistakes might cost the team the championship. The All-Stars try to help their nervous friend build his self-confidence, but it takes a pep talk from a major-league pro to get Brian back on track.

PARK ALL-STARS BY DEAN HUGHES

#5 ROOKIE STAR

Does Kenny think he's too good for his old friends? He's been seen practicing with some older players, and the local paper runs an article calling him a "rookie star." Jacob and Harlan think he's got a bad case of swollen head, and the whole team starts fighting. Can they get it together before it's too late?

#6 PRESSURE PLAY

Their rivals are playing dirty and the Dodgers are starting to lose their spirit as well as their tempers. Jacob, benched because of slipping grades, sees that it's up to him to use his brains instead of his bat to come up with a solution that will put the Dodgers back in the running for the championship. But how?

#7 LINE DRIVE

When the Dodgers' second baseman breaks his leg, no one expects that Coach Wilkens will choose little Lian Jie, a new player from the minor league, to take his place. Harlan can see that Lian Jie's got the right stuff to be a Dodger, but how can he help the new kid prove it to the rest of the team?

#8 CHAMPIONSHIP GAME

The Dodgers have a shot at the league title, but they're puzzled by Coach Wilkens's strange behavior. First he takes star slugger Rodney Bunson out of the game, and then he starts coaching players on other teams. Can the Dodgers keep their coach from wrecking their chances at the championship?

BULLSEYE BOOKS PUBLISHED BY ALFRED A. KNOPF, INC.